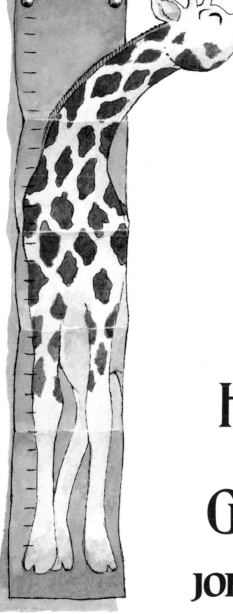

HASN'T HE GROWN!

JOHN TALBOT

Andersen Press · London

For Sarah

Copyright ©1989 by John Talbot.
This paperback edition first published in 2001 by Andersen Press Ltd. The rights of John Talbot to be identified as the author and illustrator of this work have been asserted by him in accordance with the Copyright, Designs and Patents Act, 1988.
First published in Great Britain in 1989 by Andersen Press Ltd., 20 Vauxhall Bridge Road, London SW1V 2SA.
Published in Australia by Random House Australia Pty., 20 Alfred Street, Milsons Point, Sydney, NSW 2061.
All rights reserved. Colour separated in Switzerland by Photolitho AG, Zurich.
Printed and bound in China.

10 9 8 7 6 5 4 3 2 1

British Library Cataloguing in Publication Data available.

ISBN 0 86264 232 9

This book has been printed on acid-free paper

"Hello, Marge, how are you?"
"Fine. It's lovely to see you, Beryl. Come in."

"Rachel, aren't you the pretty one? I just love
your dress."
"This must be Malcolm. I remember when you
were just a tiny, tiny baby!"

"Rachel, say 'hello' to Malcolm."
"Malcolm, why don't you show Rachel your toys?"

"Hasn't he grown!

He gets bigger and bigger every time I see him."

"Oh yes, he's got a huge appetite, our Malcolm . . .

he's practically eating us out of house and home."

"You're very lucky, Marge, our Rachel hardly eats

a thing, she just plays with her food.

Mind you, she's quite bright. She simply devours books."

"Our Malcolm is quite fond of books too,
especially ones with coloured pictures."

"Rachel's good at pictures. Give her a pencil and she'll draw anything for you."

"Malcolm is good with his hands. You should see
what he does with a few old bricks.

He's got a wonderful imagination...

we think he could be an engineer or something."

"Well, we think Rachel would make a fine nurse.

She's so caring."

"Malcolm's quite an affectionate child. He and
Bruno are great pals."

"It's funny you should say that, Marge, our Rachel
has a real way with animals.

And she's very helpful around the house.

She's a demon with the vacuum cleaner."

"We let Malcolm help with the washing-up sometimes.

He loves it, mind you... we have to keep an eye
on him."

"Rachel's just the same with water. She can be a proper little madam when she wants to!"

"Just like our Malcolm. When he's made up his
mind to do something there's no stopping him."

"I know just what you mean, Marge.
Aren't kids funny?"

"Perhaps we had better see what those two little monsters are up to!"

"Oh look! They're playing so nicely together, it's a pity we have to stop them."

"Come on, Rachel. It's time we were going home, darling."

"Goodbye!"
"Say, 'thank you for having me'."